Sister is in Teacher Jane's class. Teacher Jane has a special Valentine's Day treat for her students. There are Valentine's Day surprises hidden all around her classroom.

The cubs look around the classroom.
"Look!" says Sister. "I found a
valentine behind the globe!"

"Look!" says Lizzy. "I found a valentine behind the hamster cage!"

Now it is time for the class valentine party. Some of the cubs have valentines inside their lockers.

Some of the cubs have valentines inside their desks.

Most of the valentines are very nice.
"Here, Sister," says Lizzy. "This valentine
is for you."

"I have a valentine for you, too, Lizzy,"
says Sister.

Daffodils are yellow.
Cherry blossoms, pink.

But some of the valentines are not so nice. "Here, Sister," says Barry. "I got this special valentine for you."

Oranges are orange.
Watermelons, green.

"Thanks a lot, Barry," says Sister. "It just so happens I have a special valentine for you, too!"

"Gee thanks, Sister," says Barry. "I didn't know you cared!"

Panda Bear is black and white. Grizzly Bear is brown.

But the best valentine of all is the one that the whole class gives to Teacher Jane.

To Teacher Jane

We love our teachers at Bear Country School,